Reprint Publishing

FOR PEOPLE WHO GO FOR ORIGINALS.

www.reprintpublishing.com

ECHOES OF CHEER

ECHOES OF CHEER
JOHN KENDRICK BANGS

BOSTON
SHERMAN FRENCH & COMPANY
MDCCCCXII

Title-Page Design By
LUELLA SHAYLER HARMON

TO

THE ONLY MUSE

M. G. B.

CONTENTS

ECHOES OF CHEER

INSPIRATION

WHEN Phyllis lets me gaze into her eyes,
It fills my soul with ever fresh surprise
To note a figure small deep-set in each,
As though a thousand leagues beyond my
reach,
No larger than the tiniest woodland elf—
Each one the perfect portrait of myself.

The perfect portrait? Nay! I would 'twere
so,
Rejoicing in that soft and heavenly glow
That hedges them about! What utter bliss
To live, and be, in such a home as this,
And looking out from it each day to see
The world as Phyllis thinks the world to be!

Ah, well—let it be mine to choose my way,
Year after year, through every passing day,
So well, in truth, that as this world appears
To her, unsullied, void of evil fears,
So may it be as far as in me lies
To keep it as it seems to Phyllis' eyes!

THE IMMORTAL MUSIC

THE soft, sweet notes of woodland birds,
　　The crooning of the lowing herds,
The rustling zephyrs as they pass
Across the tree-tops and lush grass,
The humming of the bees, the throng
Of insects with their even-song,
The chirp of cricket, and the note
Of tree-toads on the air afloat,
The monotones of waters free,
The murmurs of the forest tree,
The rich crescendos of the gale,
Staccato of the rain and hail—
These are the songs our fathers stirred;
These are the songs that Adam heard;
These are the anthems that will be
Unchanged through all eternity:
The Symphony Divine that rolls
From Heaven forth to human souls,
To cheer the heart, and ease earth's strife
With promise of immortal life.

REPAYMENT

THAT part of me that from the earth hath
     come
Let earth take back again when comes the hour
That marks of my achievement the full sum,
And sets the limit to my meed of power.

I grudge no bit of it! The loan of clay
That from earth's breast I've ta'en I shall re-
     turn,
And have no least reluctance to repay,
Nor ever think the debt incurred to spurn.

But that which of the Spirit is in me
Let no earth-creditor of me demand:
To earth give earth's, to Immortality
The gifts divine from the Immortal Hand.

THE PATH

I DREAMED a fair, sweet realm
  Where all was Constancy;
With Virtue at the helm,
  And every Soul was free.
Peace smiled upon broad fields
  From Hope's fair skies above,
And all men toiled for yields
  Of Helpfulness and Love.

All eyes spoke Confidence.
  The prospect, sweeping, wide,
Breathed God's munificence
  And care on every side.
Grim Poverty was gone.
  Gone Worry and Distress,
And over all there shone
  The Light of Kindliness.

And then I woke to find
  I held Life's Golden Key.
Mine eyes that had been blind
  Were opened and could see:
Who love of service hath,
  In faith, without alloy,
Will find the blessed path
  Unto the realm of Joy!

BLIND

"SHOW me your God!" the Doubter cries.
  I point him out the smiling skies;
I show him all the woodland greens;
I show him peaceful sylvan scenes;
I show him winter snows and frost;
I show him waters tempest-tost;
I show him hills rock-ribbed and strong;
I bid him hear the thrush's song;
I show him flowers in the close—
The lily, violet, and rose;
I show him rivers, babbling streams;
I show him youthful hopes and dreams;
I show him maids with eager hearts;
I show him toilers in the marts;
I show him stars, the moon, the sun;
I show him deeds of kindness done;
I show him joy, I show him care,
And still he holds his doubting air,
And faithless goes his way, for he
Is blind of soul, and cannot see!

ANOTHER CHANCE

I WOULD that there might be
    Two lives on earth
For those of us who see
    Too late its worth.

The first, a study hour
    To learn its ways;
To comprehend the power
    Of passing days.

To find Life's deepest reach—
    The things that give
The Soul its strength, and teach
    Us how to live.

The second, that the Soul
    May nobly rise
Prepared to win the goal
    Where Honor lies.

What joy to know 'mid all
    Life's stress and pain
We but await the call
    To try again!

ON A RAINY DAY

PUTTERIN' around the house—
   That's a heap o' fun!
Sort o' snoopin' like a mouse,
   Nothin' to be done
That ye have to do at all,
   But jest lookin' round,
In the attic and the hall,
   For what may be found.

While the rain is comin' down
   With its patter song,
In an easy dressin'-gown,
   Putterin' along—
Nothin' "must" about the game,
   Not a single rule;
Idlin' like a dancin' flame
   On the log of Yule.

Mercy! All the things ye find—
   Letters old and sere
Bringin' back into your mind
   Folks no longer here;
Pictures of your school-boy pals
   In the days gone by;
Tin-types of the roguish gals
   Useter make ye sigh!

[7]

Old and yellow papers of
　　Some forgotten day;
Old forgotten tales of love
　　Long since passed away—
Maybe just a ribbon blue
　　Tangled up with tears
Bringin' back somebody you
　　Loved in Yesteryears.

Yes, indeed, the drops of rain
　　As they fall outside
Help to pleasure and to pain,
　　Humbleness and pride,
When ye putter round the house
　　In your dressin'-gown,
Like a snoopin' little mouse,
　　While it's comin' down.

ALLEGIANCE

AGE called for him and bade him come along
  And join the hoary-headed, faltering
       throng
That staggered down the hills of Life, but he
Though smiling welcome, full of courtesy,
       Replied, "Ah, no!
       I shall not go.
'Tis true my brow is furrowed deep with care,
And white as winter's drifting snow my hair;
Mine eyes and step, they too have feebler grown,
And but few days remain to call my own,
Yet there is that within my soul to-day
       That bids me tell thee Nay!
Thou hast indeed won o'er the major part,
But Youth still rules the Kingdom of my
       Heart!"

TO AN ORCHID IN A SHOP-WINDOW

POOR fragile creature! Butterfly of flowers,
    Thy span of life at most a few short
        hours,
What shame to hold thee in a prison pent,
    Thy beauty wasted on a City lane,
      Unheeded by the throngs of Toil and
        Pain,
Like some poor Poet in a tenement!

TWO LOVES

I LOVE the town because I love my fellow-
   men.
Their handiwork in admiration high I hold.
Their feats of wondrous strength, in science
   past my ken,
   Their winding boulevards, and towers tall
   and bold,
All awe my spirit as I wander idly on;
   All breathe to me a sense of striving, brawn
   and brain,
And tell a tale of vast achievement nobly won
   From bitter struggles weft of unremitting
   pain.

And yet when through the peaceful country-
   side I roam,
   Past richly verdured hills, through forests
   green and deep,
When from some mountain height beneath the
   vaulted dome
   Mine eye takes in the glory of that far-flung
   sweep,
My heart from cities turns, and all my being
   thrills
   With love, and buoyant joy, and peace, and
   ecstasy—
The town is Man's and mortal, but the dales
   and hills
   Immortal are and whisper of Divinity!

FOR LOVE OF SONG

WHAT though your songs remain unheard?
  Unheeded lie of all?
Think you that yonder lyric bird
  For this would cease his call?

He sings because he loves to sound
  His measures through the dell,
Nor cares if he be never crowned
  Because he sings them well.

So sings the Poet true alway,
  Like bird upon the wing,
Who cares not for the praise, or bay,
  But merely loves to sing.

A WISH

MY very soul I'd give
　　To write a line to live
Forever and for aye,
For in that single line
This bartered soul of mine
Would dwell, and dwelling there, would live
　　alway!

A WINTER ROSE

BLOOMED a rose one winter's day—
    Seemed to think that it was May.
Took it, I, to one I know,
One who sets my heart aglow,
Who received it with a sigh,
Held it close and tenderly,
Placed it softly on her breast;
And the flower there at rest
Till it breathed its life away
Never knew it was not May!

A DISTINCTION

FAME'S very sweet, yet we should careful be
    That it is Fame, not Notoriety.
'Tis satisfaction small, none can deny,
To be a cinder in the Public Eye.

THE MIRACLE

WHENE'ER I find my Faith grown dim,
    And all my paths seem dark and grim
    I look about me for a sign
    Of things divine,
And somewhere I am sure to see
One thing that brings it back to me:
    The love of Mother for her child;
    A wooer by a maid beguiled;
    The bond between two spirits gray
    Who hand in hand have walked the way
    From Youth to Age, and still hold fast
    Upon the love of days long past;
    The tender sympathy of Man
    For Brothers in the human clan—
Love is the Miracle I see
That brings my Faith back unto me.

AS TO NOTHING

WHO Nothing hath smiles grimly at dis-
      tress,
And cries, "I've naught to lose!" Yet, if he
      press
    On toward the height
    He'll find he is not right—
With effort he may lose his Nothingness!

GREETINGS

A BUTTERFLY came by to-day,
　　And I was glad to see
That as he sped along his way
　　He waved his wings at me.

The apple-blossoms rarely white
　　As I went idly on
Gave me a greeting of delight
　　With promised sweets anon.

Deep in the wood a silver brook
　　Ran carolling along,
And from his fern-embedded nook
　　Sent me a gift of song.

A lark flew through the upper air,
　　And with his high note clear
Bade me dismiss all thoughts of care
　　And think alone of cheer.

OUT OF THE DEPTHS

I SEE the plough cleave through the field,
　　The harrow scar the earth with pain,
And from the wound there springs a yield,
　　A harvest rich of golden grain.

I see a soul by sorrow seared,
　　A heart 'whelmed by the harrower,
And from the seeming ruin reared
　　The perfect sheaf of Character!

LOVE'S ABODE

LOVE calls at will on all who'll let him in.
　　He carries lavish gifts that all may win.
Should you be out when he doth call some day,
Or pass him by unknowing on the way,
Come hither and his smiling face you'll see—
I'm glad to say that he abides with me.

A CALL

O COME, let's all be Poets!
 What though we cannot rhyme?
'Tis easy when we know it's
 Just singing all the time;
Just sounding on the tabor
 God places in our hearts,
And taking to our neighbor
 The message He imparts.

ECHOES

I WONDER if the Heart is not
The place where Echo dwells—
Like some secluded peaceful spot
Deep-thrilled with mystic spells.

The Songs of Long Ago I seem
To hear again within;
And voices passed into a dream
Anew their measures spin.

The words of Poets passed away
Still sound their numbers there,
And turn the darkest, dullest, day
To hours of pleasure rare.

And now and then there comes to me
Deep in this Heart of mine
An echoing sense of Mystery
That hints of things Divine.

WISDOM

IF ever I am wise
　　May it not be from books,
But from the friendly skies,
　　The mountains, and the brooks—
Or possibly from eyes
　　Through which a lover looks!

No page confinéd thought
　　May this my wisdom be,
But that by Nature wrought
　　In hill, and dale, and sea—
With little flashes fraught
　　With Love's divinity.

A CHALLENGE

"COME Worry, let us walk abroad to-day.
    Let's take a little run along the way.
I know a sunny path that leads from Fear
Up to the lovely fields of Wholesome Cheer.
I'll race you there! I'm feeling fit and strong,
    So, Worry, come along!"

We started on our way, I and my Care.
I set the pace on through the spring-time air,
    But ere we'd gone a mile poor Worry
        stopped,
    Tried hard to catch his breath, and then he
        dropped,
        Whilst I sped on,
An easy winner of that Marathon.

And since that day, when vexed by any fear,
When Worry's come again with visage drear,
I've challenged him to join me in that race,
And found each time he could not stand the
        pace!

THE VALET OF THE LILY

MANY'S the task that I have had—
　　Some have been joyous, others sad;
Some have been easy, by the card;
Others at times have tried me hard;
But O what joy, and sunny hours,
To act as Valet to the Flowers!

To manicure the Roses' stem,
And carry water unto them!
To help them curl their petals rare,
And keep them ever fresh and fair—
'Tis sweet indeed to use one's powers
In valetting the fragrant Flowers!

I love to help the Garden choose
What it shall wear, and what its hues;
To keep the Pansies' faces clean,
And trim the Hedge's locks of green,
And ready make their vernal bowers
For the receptions of the Flowers.

And oh, what wages rich are mine!
Fresh currency from bush and vine,
All promptly paid when they are due
In coin that rings forever true—
No other task so richly dowers
As acting Valet to the Flowers!

[25]

A smile of welcome when I come;
A hint of pleasures frolicsome;
And when the daily task is done
A coat of tan—gift of the Sun—
And health, and silvery summer showers,
To him who serves the gracious Flowers!

AS TO DESTINY

IS it to be my destiny
　　Seeking the task too great for me?
Finding the prizes I would seek
Ever beyond, on some far peak
Out of my reach, ne'er to be won,
E'en when at last my course is run?

Then be it so! 'Tis not for me
Looking for flaws in destiny!
Still will I seek those prizes vast
Ever beyond, unwon at last!
What care I for the bitter pace?
Mine is the solace of the chase!

Joy of hope that illumes despair;
Joy of conquering woe and care;
Scent of battle, the upward flight,
On, ever onward toward the height—
These all are mine, let destiny
Hold what she may in store for me!

SOMEONE'S BIRTHDAY

TO-DAY is Someone's Birthday.   Whose
   Is all unknown to me,
But I beseech thee, O my Muse,
   All kindliness to be.

O make it bright, and richly lade
   With life's best blessings, pray,
For lad or lassie, man or maid,
   Who celebrates to-day.

If there be tears in any eyes,
   Or griefs that stir the soul,
Place o'er them thy most smiling skies,
   And ease the pangs of dole.

If there be cares that vex the mind,
   Or trials in the heart,
O Day, be gloriously kind,
   And bid all woe depart.

Upon a bitter past the Gates
   Of Lethe close, and ope
The Golden Doors to the Estates
   Of Peace, and Rest, and Hope!

WHERE THE FUN COMES IN

TO hev all things ain't suited to my mind,
    Fer, as I go my way, I seem to find
That half the fun o' life is wantin' things,
And t'other half is gittin' 'em, by Jings!

THE OPTIMIST

CARE came first and laid his siege,
   Laid his siege at my front-door;
Then the Wolf, the Lord and Liege
   Of all Trouble, brought his score.
Well, I "sicked" the Wolf on Care—
   Wolf was hungry past all doubt;
Chewed old Care up hide and hair,
   Left no sign of him about.

Then I took my faithful gun,
   Cheerfulness, from off the rack;
Loaded it with Wholesome Fun,
   Let Wolf have it front and back. .   .   .
Made a fur coat of his hide—
   He was quite a shaggy beast—
And the rest of him we fried
   For our glad Thanksgiving Feast.

AN AUTUMN REVERIE

WHEN Autumn breezes 'gin to howl
 About the chimney-pots,
And all the kine, and all the fowl,
 Seek out the sheltered spots,
I like to sit before the blaze
 And toast my shins and toes,
The while the wind its roundelays
 About the roof-tree blows.

I love to hear the windows shake,
 And listen to the sound
The rattling panes and sashes make
 As zephyrs frisk around.
I love to listen to the tune
 Of breezes in the eaves,
Commingled with the soothing croon
 Of crackling autumn leaves.

And when the logs begin to hiss
 And sputter in their ire,
I taste the joys of perfect bliss
 While sitting by the fire,
For there it seems as though the Wood
 Were sending messages
To one who shared and understood
 Its reminiscences.

AGE AND YOUTH

YOUTH takes its joys from hopeful
    dreams
  Of future prizes to be won,
Of voyages on unknown streams
  In realms beyond the rising sun.

But Age, reflective Age, delights
  E'en in the twilight's fading rays
In turning to the joyous sights
  Of unforgotten yesterdays.

I know not which more joy imparts,
  Which holds the greater thrill, the page
That tells of Hope in youthful hearts,
  Or tender memories of age.

AN OASIS

OFT in the City's byways grim
    Where joy seemed dead, and hope grown
        dim,
The laughter of a child at play
Has driven darkling thoughts away.
Poor laddy! Doomed to find your joys
In sun-baked cañons; 'mid the noise
Of barter and inhuman strife—
To pass the Maytime of your life!
Perhaps this is your message here,
To bring relief and notes of cheer,
      Like an oasis
      In desert places!

PAST, PRESENT, AND FUTURE

'TIS mighty pleasant looking back
   Through sunny vistas on life's track.
It sets the heart to beating fast
To see those visions of the past,
To hear once more the roundelays
      Of Childhood days.

'Tis fine indeed to look ahead
To see the prizes richly spread
Upon the gleaming banquet-board,
Perhaps our own deserved reward,
For these are fair, e'en though unwon,
      To look upon.

The past is full of sweetness true.
The skies of days to come are blue.
Both prospects thrill, and yet I look
Within no past or future book,
So many treasures can be found
      By looking round.

A RECIPE

THE Recipe of Youth I've found at last,
  And deeply of it now I'm daily drinking:
A thimbleful of Boyhood from the past,
  To one full quart of happy cheerful think-
    ing.

AT EVENTIDE

YES, the sun is going,
    Going, going down.
Eventide is throwing
    Shadows o'er the town;

And the stars a-gleaming,
    Gleaming over all
Unto rest and dreaming
    Soon will sound the call;

And the soft night creeping,
    Creeping o'er the way,
Guards us, guides us sleeping
    Back again to day!

TO THE TAX-ASSESSOR

COME, O Tax-Assessor Man,
　　Get your taxes if you can.
Here's the list of property
Now belonging unto me:
　One small home you may behold
　Worthier than celestial gold;
　One large heart in which there lies
　All the bliss of Paradise;
　Love of children in great store;
　Friendships reckoned by the score;
　Peaceful nights, and busy days;
　Right of way o'er golden ways;
　Jewelled sunsets, rippling seas,
　Starry skies, and cooling breeze;
　Acres broad in Fancy's realm;
　Ships with young Love at the helm;
　Freedom of the firmament;
　Endless stock of sweet content;
　Faith in God, and sturdy health—
　Thus is itemized my wealth!

Come, O Tax-Assessor-Man—
State their value if you can,
And whatever tax you lay
I will without protest pay,
On my store of Treasure-trove
In the currency of Love.

A VICTORIOUS SURRENDER

I'M praying for clear weather.
  The farmer prays for rain.
I'm thinking of the heather.
  He's thinking of his grain.
He thinks he needs the water
  To make the harvest fair.
I think of someone's daughter
  Who's waiting over there.

The point I've puzzled over
  All through the longish night,
The farmer or the lover—
  Which has the greater right?
'Twixt bread and love, I wonder,
  Which serves mankind the best?
The more and more I ponder
  The harder seems my quest.

Bread without love—what is it?
  Love without bread? Well, now
Bring on your rain—I'll visit
  Myrtilla anyhow!
And though the Atlantic Ocean
  Shall come down from the skies,
My weather, I've a notion,
  I'll find deep in her eyes.

THE SIMPLER JOYS

THERE'S joy no doubt in complicated
        things.
Much happiness I trow may come to Kings
   Who know not play, nor romp,
   But live in frigid pomp.
But when at dawn my friend who sporteth
        wings
Taps on my window-pane, and gaily sings
  His roundelay, I would not change my lot
  For all the treasure that the King hath got!

There's much of pleasure in great stores of
        wealth
If they be won by effort, not by stealth,
   By billionaires and such
   Who have the Midas touch,
But when I feel within the stir of health
That sets me high in Nature's Commonwealth,
  For all the stores of Croesus, and his line,
  I'd not exchange the treasure that is mine.

To joy in all things good, whate'er they be;
To joy in earth, the heavens, and the sea,
   And find in simple ways
   The riches of my days—
That is the test of happiness for me;
That is the measure of the life that's free.
  Let others choose the bauble with its care—
  I'll live, and be contented with my share.

THE TREASURE SEEKERS

ONE sought the East for gems, and found, alas,
Dire failure was his most unhappy pass.
One sought for pearls in waters of the Ind,
And sank a victim of the seas and wind.
Another sought the gold that glitters free
Upon the strands far in the Northern sea,
And on the beaches of that land of white
His bones lie resting in the endless night.
A fourth plunged in the nearer fray to win
The gaudy raiment that the Trade Elves spin,
And at the last found coffers full of dross—
The gold was profit, but his soul was loss!

For me, in Fortune's strife, give me the part
Of him that delves deep in the Mines of Heart—
Not far afield, but here let me secure
From them that love me treasures that endure!

THE AUCTION

HERE is Polly's heart for sale—
    Highest bidder wins!
Speak up, O ye timid male,
    Time the flying spins.
What's your offer for a heart
    Warm and full of cheer?
Let us have a bid to start!
    What's the bid I hear?

LANDS?   The bid is lands, my friends—
    Acres, broad and fine;
Full of teeming dividends
    In the harvest line.
Any higher bid? . . . O fie!
    What a sleepy band!
GOING, GOING, GOING—My!
    Heart like this for LAND?

What? A bid of GOLD? Aha!
    That's the way to bid.
Better than mere acres, far,
    That cannot be hid.
Yet, who'd win a heart like this
    With a lump of gold?
GOING, GOING—shame it is
    If it thus were sold!

Ah! Another bid comes in.
  Speak up louder—FAME?
Here's a bidder hopes to win
  With a gilded name.
But for hearts so warm and true
  That's a trifle low.
GOING—GOING! Really you
  Should not let it go!

GOING—GOING! Now, see here,
  This is bargain day.
Win a heart so full of cheer
  With a bit of bay?
Really—what's that? Speak up clear—
  Ah! We're getting on!
LOVE'S the highest bid I hear—
  GOING—
            GOING—
                    GONE!

THE USE OF LIFE

HE'D never heard of Phideas,
    He'd never heard of Byron;
His tastes were not fastidious,
His soul was not aspirin'—
But he could tell you what the birds were
        whispering in the trees;
And he could find sweet music in the sounding
        of the seas;
    And he could joy in wintry snows,
      And summer's sunny weather,
    And tell you all the names of those
      That frolic in the heather.

He'd never heard of Socrates;
He'd never heard of Irving;
He loved the mediocrities
Much more than the deserving—
But when the frost was in the air he knew the
        fox's hole;
The haunt of deer and beaver, and the wood-
        chuck and the mole;
    And he could joy in arching trees,
      In Heavens blue, or starlit,
    And in the cold crisp autumn breeze
      That paints the country scarlet.

He nothing knew of sciences,
Of art, or eke of letters;
Nor of those strange appliances
That fill the world with debtors—
But happiness he knew right well. He'd
learned from A to Z
The art of filling life with song, and others'
souls with glee;
And he could joy in day and night,
Heart full of pure Thanksgiving—
I am not sure he was not right
In using Life for living!

SCABBARD AND SWORD

THE scabbard is worn,
  But the sword is bright.
The sheath's forlorn,
  And a sorry sight.

But the blade is keen
  And its edge holds true,
And it cuts as clean
  As it used to do.

And the point is fine,
  And the steel is fair,
And it cleaves the line
  To a breadth of hair.

It is thus the Heart
  In the days untold
Will bear its part
  Though the sheath be old.

THE BECKONING YEARS

THE beckoning years are calling to me;
    They've beckoned, and beckoned, since
        infancy,
      And they seemed to say
      In that childhood day,
"Come hither and play, come play!"

And I played with them, and I romped along
With a joyous heart full of heedless song;
      And the years flew by
      With never a sigh,
Until Youth, dear Youth drew nigh.

"Come hither and learn!" was their new refrain.
I followed them over the road again
      That heroes galore
      In the days of yore
Had travailed and struggled o'er.

Then the urgent seasons, once fresh and green,
Took on a more grave and serious mien,
      And one after one
      Commanded, "My son,
Let labor be now begun!"

And I ceased my play, and I turned to toil,
And I strove for fame, and struggled for spoil;
      But the beckoning crew
      Still further drew
Me on to a love that's true.

[46]

And the years flew by and they beckoned still,
And they urged to good, and they lured to ill.
    Like the autumn leaf,
    Or the withered sheaf,
  They whispered of joy and grief.

And I grieved and grieved till my heart was
        sore,
And I joyed with a joy that was brimming
        o'er,
    All at their behest,
    And now as their guest
  They beckon me on to rest!

The peace of the childhood days was rare!
The joys of the labor and love were fair—
    For my smiles and tears,
    For my hopes and fears,
  I bless the beckoning years!

THE GARDEN OF MY DREAMS

'TIS true I love that Garden fair
　　In which I labor day by day.
'Tis happiness to lavish there
Such constant watchfulness and care
　　The while the budding posies play;
And yet there is another spot
　　Wherein the sun more brightly gleams,
Where weed and blighting cometh not,
A never-fading floral plot—
　　The wondrous Garden of my Dreams!

'Tis guarded both by day and night
　　By graceful sun-flowers, golden warm,
From which there streams a wealth of light
That keeps it ever fresh and bright,
　　And drives away the gloom of storm;
And scores of little blue-bells near,
　　While smiling pansies spout their rhymes,
Beat time to music, soft and clear,
That rings out on the atmosphere
　　Like Fairyland's Cathedral chimes.

The roses when they see me come
　　Raise up their pretty heads and smile,
And burst into a merry hum
As though they thought that I were some
　　Good friend who'd been away awhile;

And each forget-me-not I see
   At hide-and-seek in that rare place
Brings back the memory to me
Of loving smiles that used to be
   On some beloved face.

Dear Garden of my Dreams! How blest
   Art thou! How fragrant and how fair!
I'm always glad to go to rest,
And call the Sandman welcome guest
   Who nightly comes to lead me there!

A PROTEST

I WISH some big Policeman might
    Take note of Father Time,
Who runs along by day and night
    At speed that is a crime.
Why here at fifty years am I
    With heart so full of joy
That it were useless to deny
    I'm aught but just a boy!

'Tis hardly fair to go so fast
    That one runs into age
Before his spirit's really passed
    The knickerbocker stage;
To have to wear the dignity
    Of Solons grave and sad
Before one's really ceased to be
    A frisky, romping lad.

I want to shout, and sing, and dance.
    I want to frisk and play.
I want to go outside and prance
    Along the broad highway.
I want to make strange noises, but
    In spite of all I plan,
Sedately on my way I strut,
    An old stiff-mannered man!

Time plays us tricks—no doubt of that.
  He robs us of our hair;
Some folks he lays out wholly flat
  With grievous gifts of care;
But worst of all his elfish fleers,
  The meanest one, in truth,
Is when he puts the mask of Years
  Upon the face of Youth!

A PROPHECY

NO Prophet, I,
    And yet I dare to prophesy:
This coming Spring
The birds will sing,
And from her tuneful throat
    The thrush's note
      Will ring;
And blossoms fair and white
Will spring forth in the night,
To gladden some sweet day,
    In coming May;
    And roses rare
    Will scent the air,
While frolic bees their sweets will seize
And hide them in the forest trees;
And silver streams will dance along,
And babble forth their merry song
    Of mating with the sea;
The while the woodland wild will teem
With wakings from a wintry dream,
    From icy fetters free.
    Where late was snow
    The April glow
Of genial sun will melt the way
    That violet and lily pale
    May find again the ferny vale,

And Elfin comrades at their play.
The skies above
Will whisper love,
And with their dreamy blue
Will put to rout
The hosts of Doubt
And Rue!

THE HUNTER

WENT out shootin' in the wood—
My, the mornin' air was good!
Sort of filled your soul with joy.
Made ye feel jest like a boy.
Made ye want to dance, and sing
Like a wild-bird on the wing.

Soon a pattridge come along,
Whirrin', whirrin', mighty strong.
Had my gun acrost a rail,
And a bead that couldn't fail,
But, by Jings, I felt so full
Ne'er a trigger could I pull!

Later on I found a track
Leadin' through the piney black,
Surest thing ye ever knew—
Mr. Fox had jest been through—
Trailed him squarely to his hole—
Couldn't shoot to save my soul!

'N'en I heerd a tromplin' sound,
Like a big deer some'ers round;
'N'en a cracklin' in the bush,
'N'en a sudden sort o' hush,
An' a pair o' starin' eyes
Soft as ever summer skies.

Shoot him? I'd as soon ha' shot
Sleepin' babies in a cot.
Kill him? With two eyes a-beam
With a sort o' friendly gleam?
Nary kill for Mr. Deer
In that mornin' atmosphere!

So it went the whole day long.
Somepin sort o' went all wrong.
Had my gun, and had my lead,
Got up early out o' bed
For to land a lot o' things,
And jest couldn't—no, by Jings!

HALLOWE'EN

BRING forth the raisins and the nuts—
    To-night All-Hallow's Spectre struts
        Along the moonlit way.
No time is this for tear or sob,
Or other woes our joys to rob,
But night for pippin and for bob,
        And Jack-o'-Lantern gay.

Come forth ye lass and trousered kid,
From prisoned Mischief raise the lid,
        And lift it good and high.
Leave grave old Wisdom in the lurch,
Set Folly on a lofty perch,
Nor fear the awesome rod of birch
        When dawn illumes the sky.

'Tis night for revel, set apart
To reillume the darkened heart,
        And rout the hosts of dole.
'Tis night when Goblin, Elf, and Fay,
Come dancing in their best array,
To prank and royster on their way,
        And ease the troubled soul.

The ghosts of all things past parade,
Emerging from the mist and shade
     That hid them from our gaze;
And full of song, and ringing mirth,
In one glad moment of rebirth,
Again they walk the ways of earth
     As in the ancient days.

The beacon light shines on the hill,
The will-o'-wisps the forests fill
     With flashes filched from noon;
And witches on their broom-sticks spry
Speed here and yonder in the sky,
And lift their strident voices high
     Unto the Hunter's Moon.

The air resounds with tuneful notes
From myriads of straining throats,
     All hailing Folly Queen;
So join the swelling choral throng,
Forget your sorrow, and your wrong,
In one glad hour of joyous song
     To honor Hallowe'en!

CHRISTMAS DAY

A DAY of respite, this!
    A day of purest bliss
Wherein in Love to plan
    Good-will to Man.

A Festival of Joys
Wherein no thing annoys;
A time of Cheer and Mirth,
    And Peace on Earth.

A time for Smiles and play,
And yet withal a day
For thoughtful deeds, and good,
    Of Brotherhood.

A day for sunny rifts,
A day for loving gifts,—
For Kindness bounteous,
    God gave it us.

DISCOVERY

THE fairest voyage man can make,
  Exploring land or sea,
Is one which every Spring I take—
  My quest, Discovery.
I do not seek uncharted lands,
  Or continents unknown—
I leave that sort of things to hands
  More expert than my own.

The things I seek are simple things,
  And simple is my crew—
Myself, and One who ever sings
  A song that's sweet and true;
And as our little bark doth pass
  Along some sylvan scene
'Tis fine to learn anew that grass
  Is tender, lush and green.

'Tis joyous to discover, too,
  The while we drift along,
That skies and seas are deeply blue,
  That birds have gift of song;
To learn again that little bees
  Find honey in the flowers,
And that rich blossoms deck the trees
  In early Springtime hours;

That wild-flowers flirt with sunbeams fair;
    And in the garden-close
The fragrance of the soft spring air
    Is rifled from the rose;
To learn that trout lurk in the pool,
    And hear amid the hush
When night comes on with shadows cool
    The lyric of the thrush!

THE STORY THAT NEVER ENDS

HE told the old, old story,
 And told it mighty well.
Her face was flushed with glory
 Beneath its magic spell.
To her 'twas fresh and novel;
 To her 'twas new and sweet,
And glorified the hovel
 In which they chanced to meet.

She gave the old, old answer—
 The answer Adam got
When that primeval man, sir,
 Asked Eve to share his lot.
Amid the same old blushes
 That tinge a maiden's cheek,
Amid the same old hushes
 His riches he did seek.

They had the same old raptures
 That to the lover come
When his successful captures
 At e'en he bringeth home.
And soon the same old prattle
 Was heard within their door,
And still the same old rattle
 Upon the nursery floor.

And still the same old newness
  That makes the old things fair,
The same old joys, and blueness,
  That greet us everywhere.
The same old days of gladness,
  The same old hours of grief;
The same old times of sadness,
  The same old sweet relief.

The same old spells of weather
  To light or dim the day.
The same old age together,
  The same old locks of gray—
And though old things pursue them,
  The eyes they see them through,
Love-lit, forever view them
  Imperishably new!

"ME AND MINE"

IT'S blitherin' cold outside,
  And blowin' to beat the band;
And snow and sleet is a-flyin' wide
  Over the whole broad land.
The icicles hang from the eaves,
  And the ponds and the brooks is froze;
The frost has withered the autumn leaves
  And bit up the farmer's nose—
      But me an' mine
      Is feelin' fine,
  So what do we care for snows?

There isn't a bird in sight,
  And even the cat stays in,
Desertin' the joys of night,
  And the call of her kith and kin.
The days they are short and chill,
  The nights are a decade long,
And out on the bleak and distant hill
  The blizzard is goin' strong—
      But me an' mine
      Is feelin' fine,
  For our hearts is full o' song.

Her heart is singin' of me,
  And mine is singin' of her!
No thinkin' of what's to be,
  No thinkin' of things that were,
But just of the joys that is,
  Not worried 'bout things that's not;
So let the hoary old blizzard blizz
  And Boreas go it hot—
        For me an' mine
        Is feelin' fine,
And thankful for what we've got!

ARCADY

STARTED out for Arcady,
  No one knew the way;
Wandered onward wearily
  Through the dreary day.
Lost my bearings, lost my chart,
  Troubles round me pressed;
Footsore, weary, faint of heart,
  Spirit sore distressed.

Road to Fame was sweet indeed,
  Road to Wealth was bold.
But the laurel turned to weed,
  And the gems were cold.
Wealth and Honor are a goal
  Fit for chivalry,
But they never lead the soul
  Into Arcady.

Suddenly across my path
  Flashed a pair of eyes!
Oh, such eyes as Some One hath,
  Soft as summer skies—
Flashed like stars of summer nights
  O'er the summer sea.
Quoth my heart, "These are the lights,
  Lights of Arcady!"

Came the note of Some One's voice
  Sounding through the dark,
Singing numbers rare and choice
  As the morning lark.
Fled away the darkness all
  As it came to me.
Quoth my soul, "This is the call,
  Call of Arcady!"

At my threshold, waiting there,
  Radiant with grace,
Glint of gold upon her hair,
  Sunshine in her face;
Dancing gaily as a gnome,
  Arms stretched forth for me—
Then it was I knew that Home,
  Home was Arcady!